P9-DXT-540

THE AMAZING ADVENTURES OF THE DC SUPER-PETS!

Robin Robin to the Rescue

by **Steve Korté**

illustrated by **Art Baltazar**

Batman created by Bob Kane
with Bill Finger

PICTURE WINDOW BOOKS
a capstone imprint

Published by Picture Window Books, an imprint of Capstone.
1710 Roe Crest Drive
North Mankato, Minnesota 56003
www.capstonepub.com

Copyright © 2021 DC Comics.
DC SUPER-PETS and all related characters and elements © & ™ DC Comics.
WB SHIELD: ™ & © Warner Bros. Entertainment Inc. (s21)

All rights reserved. No part of this publication may be reproduced in whole or
in part, or stored in a retrieval system, or transmitted in any form or by any
means, electronic, mechanical, photocopying, recording, or otherwise, without
written permission of the publisher.

Library of Congress Cataloging-in-Publication Data
Names: Korté, Steve, author. | Baltazar, Art, illustrator.
Title: Robin Robin to the rescue / by Steve Korté ; illustrated by Art Baltazar.
Description: North Mankato, Minnesota : Picture Window Books, an imprint
of Capstone, [2021] | Series: The amazing adventures of the DC super-pets |
Audience: Ages 5–7. | Audience: Grades K–1. | Summary: "The Penguin, the
Joker, and Catwoman are causing trouble in Gotham City at the same time!
Robin Robin and the Boy Wonder swing into action. Will they be able to
rescue the zoo's penguins, return stolen jewelry, and stop the bank from being
robbed, all on the same night?"—Provided by publisher.
Identifiers: LCCN 2020037782 (print) | LCCN 2020037783 (ebook) | ISBN
9781515882565 (library binding) | ISBN 9781515883654 (paperback) | ISBN
9781515892212 (pdf)
Subjects: CYAC: Robins—Fiction. | Superheroes—Fiction.
Classification: LCC PZ7.K8385 Rob 2021 (print) | LCC PZ7.K8385 (ebook) |
DDC [E]—dc23
LC record available at https://lccn.loc.gov/2020037782
LC ebook record available at https://lccn.loc.gov/2020037783

Designed by Ted Williams
Design Elements by Shutterstock/SilverCircle

TABLE OF CONTENTS

He is a high-flying hero.

He fights crime in Gotham City.

He is Robin's loyal helper.

These are . . .

THE AMAZING ADVENTURES OF

Robin Robin the Bird Wonder!

Triple Threat

The sound of a triple-level crime

alarm echoes inside the Batcave.

Robin rushes to the Batcomputer. His tiny crime-fighting bird partner, Robin Robin, flies over to help.

"Uh-oh," Robin says. He looks at the screen. "Three of Gotham City's most dangerous villains are loose."

The Penguin has freed the penguins at the Gotham City Zoo. Catwoman has stolen a rare cat-shaped gem from a jewelry store. And the Joker has robbed a bank. He is getting away in his Jokermobile.

Robin hops on his motorcycle and zooms out of the Batcave. Robin Robin follows.

The two heroes arrive outside the zoo. The Penguin jumps out in front of them. He points his umbrella at Robin.

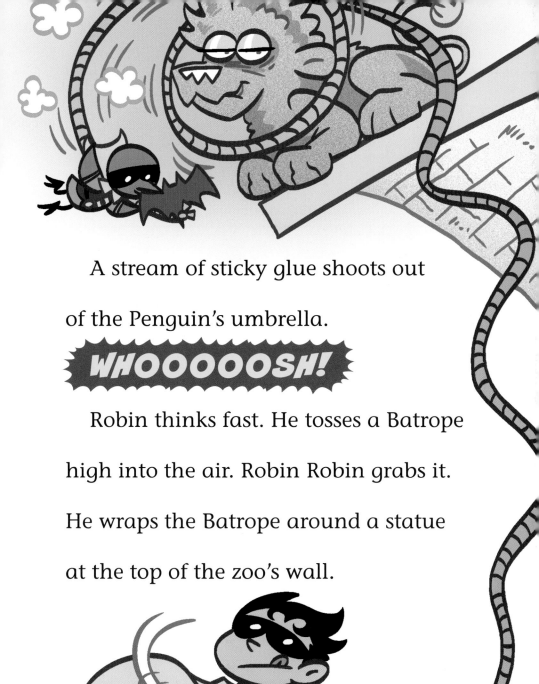

A stream of sticky glue shoots out

of the Penguin's umbrella.

WHOOOOOOSH!

Robin thinks fast. He tosses a Batrope

high into the air. Robin Robin grabs it.

He wraps the Batrope around a statue

at the top of the zoo's wall.

Robin swings through the air on the Batrope. The glue misses the Boy Wonder. It splashes onto the ground.

Robin flies over the villain and lands behind him.

"Ack!" cries the Penguin. He spins around and topples over.

The Penguin is stuck to the glue!

"Now it's time to catch Catwoman,"
says Robin.

Robin speeds away. Robin Robin
herds the penguins back into the zoo
before taking off.

CHAPTER 2

Catch the Climbing Cat!

Catwoman lives at the top of a tall skyscraper.

The two heroes burst through the apartment door. They hear the sound of breaking glass.

"Look at that hole in the window," says Robin. "Catwoman must have jumped when she saw us!"

Robin ties a Batrope near the broken window. Both boy and bird jump through.

Robin finds a bag of sand on the sidewalk.

"This was what made the hole in the window," he says. "Catwoman is still up in her apartment!"

Robin Robin rushes to the top floor

as fast as he can fly.

He gets there in time to see

Catwoman climbing onto the roof!

Robin Robin quickly wraps the

dangling Batrope around Catwoman.

She is trapped! Only one villain is left!

Eyes on the Road

The Joker's car is speeding down the streets. He sees Robin in the rear-view mirror. The Joker throws a can of green laughing gas behind him.

The laughing gas lands in the middle of the road. Robin does not see it in time. He drives right through the cloud of gas!

Robin has to stop his motorcycle. He is laughing too hard to drive.

Robin Robin flies in circles around his partner at lightning-fast speed. Thanks to his quick moves, the laughing gas clears away.

The Joker looks in the mirror and sees the heroes chasing him.

The Joker doesn't watch where he is driving. He is too close to the Gotham City harbor!

The Jokermobile sails off the dock.

SPLASH!

The car sinks into the water.

"Help! Help!" cries the Joker.

Robin Robin pulls a Batrope from his Utility Belt. He ties one end of the rope to the dock. He tosses the other end into the water.

The Joker uses the Batrope to climb out of the harbor.

Robin Robin grabs the Batrope. He flies around the Joker, looping in and out and around. He pulls the rope tight.

The Super-Pet hands the end of the rope to Robin. Then he lands on the Boy Wonder's shoulder.

"It looks like three villains are no match for a very smart Bird Wonder," says Robin.

AUTHOR!

Steve Korté is the author of many books for children and young adults. He worked at DC Comics for many years, editing more than 600 books about Superman, Batman, Wonder Woman, and the other heroes and villains in the DC Universe. He lives in New York City with his husband, Bill, and their super-cat, Duke.

ILLUSTRATOR!

Famous cartoonist Art Baltazar is the creative force behind *The New York Times* bestselling, Eisner Award-winning DC Comics' Tiny Titans; co-writer for Billy Batson and the Magic of Shazam, Young Justice, Green Lantern Animated (Comic); and artist/co-writer for the awesome Tiny Titans/Little Archie crossover, Superman Family Adventures, Super Powers, and Itty Bitty Hellboy! Art is one of the founders of Aw Yeah Comics comic shop and the ongoing comic series. Aw yeah, living the dream! He stays home and draws comics and never has to leave the house! He lives with his lovely wife, Rose, sons Sonny and Gordon, and daughter, Audrey! AW YEAH MAN! Visit him at www.artbaltazar.com

"Word Power"

crime (KRYM)—an activity that is wrong or illegal

dangling (DANG-guhl-ing)—hanging loosely

dock (DAHK)—a place where ships load and unload their supplies

harbor (HAR-bur)—a body of water next to land where ships may stop

herd (HURD)—to gather and move a group of animals

loyal (LOY-uhl)—being true to something or someone

skyscraper (SKY-skray-puhr)—a very tall building made of steel, concrete, and glass

villain (VIL-uhn)—a wicked, evil, or bad person who is often a character in a story

WRITING PROMPTS

1. Write part of the story from a villain's point of view. Will you be Catwoman, the Penguin, or the Joker?

2. Create an ad for the Penguin's glue, Catwoman's sandbag dummy, or the Joker's laughing gas. What features do these products have that regular people might find useful?

3. Draw a warning sign for the Gotham City harbor. What part of the harbor would you warn people about?

DISCUSSION QUESTIONS

1. Why do you think Robin went after the bad guys in the order he did? Would you have chased another villain first? Why?

2. Robin Robin does not have any superpowers. But he still manages to save the day! Re-read the story and make a list of his heroic actions.

3. Teamwork is important. List some ways Robin and his Super-Pet work together.